THE OCTOPUS AND THE PIRATES

THE OCTOPUS AND THE PIRATES

Mario Soldati

Pictures by ALBERTO LONGONI

André Deutsch

Once, a long time ago, there was a village in Italy called Tellaro, which is still there today. The village is built on the rocks at the foot of a promontory jutting out into the sea, and behind it rises a great hill covered with olive groves. Sheltered by the promontory there is a little creek, safe from storms, in which, long ago, the villagers built a harbour. The people who live in Tellaro, by the way, are called Tellarini.

Nowadays nearly all the men in Tellaro are sailors. They work on big ships and travel all over the world.

But, once upon a time, before steamships were invented, they were fishermen and farmers. When the sea was calm they went fishing and if it was stormy they worked in their olive groves on the big hill behind the village. They were quite well off, because they sold the fish they caught and the oil which they crushed from the olives in their olive groves to the people of a neighbouring town.

And yet their lives were never completely peaceful, because in those days the villages by the sea were in constant danger from pirates. Pirates were unscrupulous; they sailed the seas in light, fast ships with enormous sails.

They came ashore quite unexpectedly, descending on the smallest, most isolated, most defenceless villages. Villages like Tellaro. They stole everything they could carry off. They emptied the shops and the houses, they robbed women of their jewels and, it is said, even took away children who were afterwards sold as slaves. If anybody dared to resist, the pirates killed them without hesitation. Sometimes, if the villagers had fought hard, they would set fire to the houses out of revenge.

All along the coast the villagers decided that the only way to defend themselves from the pirates was to build look-out towers. They put them on the hills high above the villages and kept watch over the sea by day and by night. The alarm was given as soon as a pirate ship was sighted. In Tellaro the villagers would ring the church bells as a warning. Since sailing ships, even when the wind was favourable, could never be as fast as ships with engines, the plan often succeeded. The people of the villages had time to arm themselves and call for help from neighbouring towns. To the pirates surprise, time and again they were driven back into the sea.

The Tellarini, like everyone else, were always on their guard, always on the look-out. Their village, built high on the rocks above the sea, was a natural fortress; every house had a window through which a watch was kept.

As for the harbour it was no more than a sheltered slipway jutting out from between the houses. It was so easy to defend that all the villagers had to do was hide in their doorways and take pot shots at the pirates with their arquebuses.

One winter's evening a terrible storm blew up. The sea thundered and beat against the cliffs. The huge waves crashed against the rocks, and spray battered the houses. The fishing boats were hauled so far up the slipway that they were almost inside the houses. The sailors lashed them to the iron gratings of the windows with the strongest knots they could tie. Happy that their boats were safe the sailors took no notice of the stormy sunset which gave a menace to the dark hills towering above the harbour, and cast a strange yellow light over the waters.

They ate their supper and went early to bed. They were not dismayed by the roar of the waves, nor the lurid sky. They were used to it; and moreover they knew that a storm was their best defence against pirates. So confident were they that no one bothered to keep watch that night. Not even the devil himself could have got ashore in such a storm.

Another thing which made them feel happy was the bumper olive crop which they had just harvested. The oil jars were fuller than ever before. Whether or not they would be able to sell it all was a problem for another day.

Towards midnight, the rain began to fall. It was then that, suddenly, the bells of the little church began to ring – ding-dong, ding-dong, ding-dong, ding-dong.

In a few seconds the Tellarini are awake. They strain their ears, listening. Ding-dong, ding-dong, ding-dong. What is happening? They run to the church. The thunder cracks, the lightning flashes, a slanting rain falls in sheets, the storm rages on. They reach the bell tower and open the little door. The bells ring on. Clang, clash, clang. But, incredibly, there is no bell-ringer. The bell tower is empty. The bells are ringing themselves. Even the ropes are nowhere to be seen.

In the light from a streak of lightning the villagers see the bell ropes hanging outside the bell tower, an enormous octopus clinging to them, pulling desperately with his eight sinewy tentacles;
helped in his grim struggle by the waves which toss him helplessly to and fro.

At that moment
another flash of
lightning gives the

villagers a glimpse of two sails streaking into the harbour. Pirates! The Tellarini are at a loss. There is no time to get help, and they can think of no way to defend themselves. Then someone remembers the bumper olive crop and it gives him an idea. In a trice as many jars as they can carry are piled up in the doorways. The oil is poured into great copper pots and a big fire is hastily lit underneath each one. The pirates draw near. The Tellarini wait silently, keeping the fires roaring. The pirates creep ashore, peering suspiciously into the darkness.

At just the right moment the signal is given and, as one man, the Tellarini empty the pots of boiling oil over the pirates beneath them.

You can imagine what happens next. The pirates hurl themselves into the sea, not so much to get back to their ships as to cool off.

At the same time the Tellarini shoulder their arquebuses and fire. Never has any village, under attack from pirates, achieved so complete a victory.

To this day an octopus, skilfully designed in slate, can be seen on the wall of the little church in Tellaro above the porch. It reminds the Tellarini of their saviour.

There are some, however, who insist that the whole thing was only co-incidence. What they think happened is this: On that night the wind blew so strongly that it wrenched the bell ropes through the window of the tower, the pull of the surf was so strong that the octopus lost his grip on the rocks and was hurled up towards the tower. He caught hold of the ropes and clung to them to save himself from being dashed to pieces. For a while, as the waves thrust him backwards and forwards it looked as if he would lose his grip and be sucked down into the turbulent depths of the ocean. But the octopus, battling against the power of the waves, held on grimly, and as he was tossed hither and thither, so he pulled the ropes and kept the bells ringing out their warning. The fact that the octopus was struggling to stay alive at the very moment that the pirates were planning their attack on the harbour was just a happy co-incidence for Tellaro. That's what some people think.

Whether the Tellarini were saved by the courage and kindness of the octopus or by a lucky chance no one will ever know. But one thing is certain, no village has a more beautiful reminder of a great victory than the village of Tellaro.